Roberto and the Fountain of Lights

Donna Reid Vann
Illustrated by John Haysom

A LION BOOK
Tring • Batavia • Sydney

In the sunny city of Barcelona, Spain, there lived a boy whose name was Roberto. The children on his street had nicknamed him "Roberto of the Roses." This was because he bore, on one side of his face, a mark that looked like three red roses.

This mark had been there ever since Roberto was born. Nothing could hide it; nothing could take it away.

"Roberto of the Roses!
Roberto of the Roses!"

The shouts of the other children reached his ears each day as he walked down the street. He paid little attention to the teasing. His father loved him; his mother loved him, and his sister Laia thought him the most wonderful of older brothers.

Roberto was happy enough, in his life in the bustling city. From the window of his tiny bedroom near the old Gothic Quarter he could glimpse the glittering green sea. Often he would wander shoulder-to-shoulder with the crowds, up and down the broad boulevard called *Las Ramblas*, always stopping near the stalls hung with cages of parakeets for sale. Pigeons clustered on the roofs of these stalls, drawn by the chirps of captive comrades.

Roberto felt sorry for the caged birds. He would touch his finger to the door of a cage, longing to fling it open and watch the parakeet soar to the heavens. He did not dare really to set the bird free. The stall-keeper would yell at him and demand money, and Roberto had none. But since ideas cost nothing, he would let the bird go free in his thoughts. In his mind he watched as it flew upward toward the sun.

Near *Las Ramblas* were many fine shops, but he never dared to enter them. The sunny boulevard was the proper place for such a one as Roberto of the Roses, a boy who was different.

One day, however, there arose in Roberto's heart the longing for something higher than his simple existence.

"I am not happy," he said to himself, though he did not know why.

He decided to do something he had never done before. He walked to the top of the boulevard and went through the automatic sliding doors into the largest department store in Barcelona.

Roberto stood stock-still. He had never seen such a magnificent place. Everyone seemed rich and exceedingly happy. They moved in laughing little clusters, chattering excitedly over their purchases.

Hardly anyone in the store seemed to notice the boy with the red-scarred face. Only the sales ladies eyed him sharply, knowing he was not there to buy. He jostled along with the multitude, letting his upturned face brush the back of a luxurious fur coat. The touch of soft fur and the scent of the lady wearing it dazed him briefly. He stumbled carelessly through the aisles, bumping into people until he crashed against a counter and came to his senses.

After that day, Roberto returned again and again to the grand store. He liked to stand in the toy department and watch the children. They were dressed in the latest fashions and wore real leather shoes. Their skin was smooth, their hair expertly cut at the best salons.

Most of all, Roberto admired the children with curly brown hair and skin like coffee with milk. That was what his mother drank each morning; each morning as he watched her drink it, he thought of these flawless children.

"Roberto of the Roses!
Roberto of the Roses!"

Roberto began to be bothered by the continual chanting of the others. He saw the shouting group staring at him and he looked quickly away.

Why did they never ask him to play with them? Was it simply because of his face?

Roberto blushed so red that the roses were almost hidden.

One summer evening Roberto was walking aimlessly through the streets of Barcelona, feeling sad and lonely. He turned down an unfamiliar street, when suddenly he gasped in wonder.

High on a hill above him stood a brightly lit palace, with dozens of steps leading up to it. At the foot of the steps played an enormous fountain, the largest he had ever seen.

The fountain was constantly changing, in the most mysterious way. While Roberto stood transfixed, it turned now as green as the northern lights, now as purple as enchanted kingdoms, now as gold as a king's treasure.

Roberto raced toward the fountain. It threw its water high into the air in stiff soldierly spikes. By the time he had reached the fountain's base, it had transformed itself into a sparkling mist, letting the wind blow it wispily wherever it would.

Roberto stood in awe at the foot of the magical fountain. The unnamed longing welled up in him and burst open. As he gazed upon that towering beauty, he felt all at once how ugly the mark on his face truly was.

He would have bowed his head in shame, except that the fountain drew his eyes upward to its sprays, flowering above him more gloriously than spring.

For the first time, he wanted with all the strength of his heart to be just like everyone else. He wished he could leap into the waters of the fountain and let their purples and greens and golds wash away his birthmark.

After that, Roberto of the Roses was no longer content to stay in on Saturday evenings at his home, or to go out walking with his family. Instead, he returned each week to the fountain of lights. He would stand before it, feeling its spray on his face, letting its lights dazzle him, enchant him.

An old lady who sold yo-yos at the foot of the fountain noticed the boy with the roses gleaming on his cheek. She began to greet him whenever she saw him, and a friendship grew up between the two. They shared much in common, for she was old and hunched and not at all lovely.

Saturday after Saturday Roberto would leave his home just after supper and venture forth into the dark streets. Laia stood in the doorway and watched until he disappeared around a corner, wondering what drew her beloved brother away from their family circle.

He knew that she wondered and he did not care. He had to go to the fountain. He was beginning to think of it as *his* fountain. He began to believe that the fountain had magical powers.

"If I just stand under it long enough," he said to himself, "it will make my skin like that of the others."

But every night he went sadly home, with the splotches standing out on his cheek just as before.

Every day he heard the same shouting from the others:

"Roberto of the Roses!
Roberto of the Roses!"

One evening, as Roberto stood spell-bound beneath the splashing brilliant waters, it came to him that he should ask the fountain for help. With the bright roses on his face, he felt like one of the poor parakeets, trapped in its wire cage. The magical fountain surely must have the power to set him free.

As he was thinking this, the hunchbacked yo-yo lady stopped and greeted him. Her beady eyes flashed in the changing light, and suddenly she spoke in a harsh tone:

"What you are doing is wrong – wrong! The fountain cannot help you. Go to the Master Artist! Go to the Master Artist!"

Then she hobbled off, calling out as before, "Yo-yos! Who will buy my yo-yos!"

Her words troubled Roberto, though he did not understand them. Who was this Master Artist? Did she mean the artist who had designed the fountain? And where would he find such a high personage?

Roberto began to walk around the circle of the fountain, his thoughts confused. On his second time around he noticed a man standing at an easel set up in the strong light of a nearby souvenir stall. The man was gazing intently at the fountain and applying paints to a canvas resting on the easel.

An artist! If he were not the Master Artist, perhaps he would at least know where to find him.

Roberto came up behind the man and tugged gently at his sleeve.

"Please sir – are you the Master Artist?" he asked.

The man looked down, distracted by the voice at his elbow. He had a kind, merry face, and he laughed a laugh that broke in the middle at the sight of Roberto's blushing birthmark.

After a moment the man said quietly, "No. I am only an artist. There are many greater, and one who is greatest of all."

"I must find him," said Roberto. "Do you know where he is? I want so much not to be ugly any more."

At first the man looked astonished, but at last he laughed again, more merrily than before. He set down his paintbrush and took Roberto by the arm.

"Oh yes," he said, "I know this Master Artist. I can help you find him, and he will make you beautiful."

He began to walk with Roberto on his arm around and around the fountain. As they walked, he told Roberto of the Master Artist. While the man was talking, wonderful pictures came into Roberto's mind.

He pictured a world of dark nothingness, into which the Master Artist breathed all the light and beauty of nature.

He pictured a world bursting forth green. The Master Artist spoke, and fish and birds and animals of every description appeared, more and more until the earth was full.

He pictured the Master Artist making with loving care a man and a woman, to be master and mistress over his world.

During many evenings by the fountain, the artist put images of great beauty and mystery into Roberto's mind. But the most wonderful of all was this: the Master Artist, with his own hands, forming the figure of a certain boy who lives in Barcelona.

"Is it true?" asked Roberto with shining eyes, when he realized what this last picture meant. "Did the Master Artist really make me?"

The kind man nodded vigorously. "It's true," he said. "The Creator made you and he loves you very much. In his eyes you are beautiful just as you are – even to the roses on your face."

Roberto felt he would burst with joy. He began to dance and sing: "I am Roberto of the Roses! I am Roberto of the Roses!"

The passers-by stared with only a little astonishment, for things such as this could happen in Barcelona. The old lady grinned until her hooked nose and hooked chin almost touched each other.

The next day Roberto of the Roses was still dancing and singing. He danced down the street, calling proudly to the other children, "I am Roberto of the Roses! The Master Artist made me just like this. You're each different, too – have you noticed? That's because he made you that way!"

The children gaped in astonishment for a moment. Then they began to laugh and clap.

"Roberto of the Roses! Roberto of the Roses!" they shouted. "Come and play with us today!"

Roberto heard the liking in their voices and he felt warm all the way down to his dancing toes.

AFTERWORD

Nearly all of us have something about ourselves that we don't like. Perhaps it is nothing as noticeable as the red roses on Roberto's cheek. On the other hand, it may be something quite obvious, which we think makes us different from other people. We may wish that we could change it, but we cannot.

God's heart is so big that he sees everyone in his creation as beautiful. Each of us has great value in his eyes. Roberto learned to like himself when he saw that God loves him exactly as he is.

Wouldn't it be boring if we were all merely copies of one another? Let's enjoy being one of a kind – one of the Master Artist's special creations!

If you happen to be in Barcelona, and visit the National Palace on Montjuich on certain evenings, you can see Roberto's magical fountain.